ABOUT THE BANK STREET READY-TO-READ SERIES

Seventy years of educational research and innovative teaching have given the Bank Street College of Education the reputation as America's most trusted name in early childhood education.

Because no two children are exactly alike in their development, we have designed the *Bank Street Ready-to-Read* series in three levels to accommodate the individual stages of reading readiness of children ages four through eight.

- *Level 1:* GETTING READY TO READ—read-alouds for children who are taking their first steps toward reading.
- *Level 2:* READING TOGETHER—for children who are just beginning to read by themselves but may need a little help.
- *Level 3:* I CAN READ IT MYSELF—for children who can read independently.

Our three levels make it easy to select the books most appropriate for a child's development and enable him or her to grow with the series step by step. The *Bank Street Ready-to-Read* books also overlap and reinforce each other, further encouraging the reading process.

We feel that making reading fun and enjoyable is the single most important thing that you can do to help children become good readers. And we hope you'll be a part of Bank Street's long tradition of learning through sharing.

The Bank Street
College of Education

For my mother, Winifred Vanderwerp,
with love and admiration—M.M.

A Lucas • Evans Book

HEDGEHOG BAKES A CAKE
A Bantam Little Rooster Book
Simultaneous paper-over-board and trade paper editions/September 1990

Little Rooster is a trademark of Bantam Books,
a division of Bantam Doubleday Dell Publishing Group, Inc.

Library of Congress Cataloging-in-Publication Data
Macdonald, Maryann.
Hedgehog bakes a cake / by Maryann Macdonald; illustrated by
Lynn Munsinger.
p. cm.
(Bank Street ready-to-read)
"A Bantam little rooster book."
Summary: As Hedgehog starts to make a cake, his friends stop by,
one by one, and each has advice for the project.
ISBN 0-553-05872-X
ISBN 0-553-34890-6 (pbk.)
[1. Cakes—Fiction. 2. Baking—Fiction. 3. Animals—Fiction.]
I. Munsinger, Lynn, ill. II. Title. III. Series.
PZ7.M1486He   1990
[E]—dc20   89-39471
CIP
AC

Published simultaneously in the United States and Canada

Bantam Books are published by Bantam Books, a division of Bantam Dou-
bleday Dell Publishing Group, Inc. Its trademark, consisting of the words
"Bantam Books" and the portrayal of a rooster, is Registered in U.S. Patent
and Trademark Office and in other countries. Marca Registrada. Bantam
Books, 666 Fifth Avenue, New York, New York 10103.

PRINTED IN THE UNITED STATES OF AMERICA

WAK 0 9 8 7 6 5 4 3 2 1

Bank Street Ready-to-Read™

HEDGEHOG
Bakes a Cake

by Maryann Macdonald
Illustrated by Lynn Munsinger

A BANTAM LITTLE ROOSTER BOOK

NEW YORK · TORONTO · LONDON · SYDNEY · AUCKLAND

Hedgehog was hungry for cake.
He found a yellow cake recipe.
"This one sounds easy," he said,
"and good, too."

Hedgehog took out the flour.
He took out the eggs and the butter.

He was taking out the blue mixing bowl
when he heard a knock at the door.
It was Rabbit.
"Hello, Rabbit," said Hedgehog.
"I am making a cake."

"I will help you," said Rabbit.
"I am good at making cakes."
"Here is the recipe," said Hedgehog.
"You do not need this recipe," Rabbit said.
"I will show you what to do."

Rabbit took the flour.
He dumped it into the blue bowl.
He took the butter
and dumped that in, too.
Then he dumped in the sugar.
"Now we will mix it,"
said Rabbit.

Mixing was hard work.
Rabbit mixed and mixed.
His arm began to hurt.
The batter was lumpy.
The sugar stuck to the sides of the bowl.
There was flour everywhere.

"I think someone is calling me,"
said Rabbit.
"You finish the mixing, Hedgehog.
I will come back
when the cake is ready."

Hedgehog shook his head.
The cake batter was a mess.

"What's the matter, Hedgehog?"
Squirrel was at the door, looking in.
"I am making a cake," said Hedgehog.
"But it does not look very good."
"You need eggs," said Squirrel.
"I will put them in."

He cracked some eggs
and dropped them in.
Some shell fell in, too.
"A little bit of shell does not matter,"
said Squirrel.
"Mix it all together."
So Hedgehog mixed.
The batter was more lumpy,
but mixing was easier than before.

Owl stuck her head in the door.
"Baking?" she asked. "May I help?"
Hedgehog did not want more help.
But he didn't want to hurt Owl's feelings.

"You can butter the pan,"
said Hedgehog.
Owl was happy.
She stuck her wing into the butter.
Then she smeared it around the pan.

Owl turned on the oven
with her buttery feathers.
She turned it up as high as it would go.
"The oven must be nice and hot,"
she said.

"We have gotten very messy
helping you," said Squirrel.
"We will go home now and clean up.
Put the cake in the oven.
We will come back when it is ready."
Squirrel and Owl went home.

Hedgehog looked at the kitchen.
There was sugar on the floor.
There was butter on the oven door.
And there was flour on everything.

Hedgehog dumped the cake batter
into the garbage pail.
He locked the kitchen door
and took out his recipe.

First Hedgehog measured the sugar.
He mixed it slowly with the butter.
Next he counted out three eggs
and cracked them into the bowl—
one, two, three.
Then he added the flour.

Hedgehog mixed everything together
and poured it into Owl's buttery pan.

He turned down the heat
and put the batter in the oven.
Then he cleaned up the kitchen.

Knock, knock, knock.
"Open the door, Hedgehog,"
called Rabbit.
"We can smell the cake,
and we are getting hungry."
Hedgehog unlocked the door.
The kitchen was clean.
The cake was cooling on a rack.
And the table was set for a tea party.

The four friends sat down.
Hedgehog cut the cake.

They each ate one slice.
Then they each ate another slice.
"This is the best cake
I have ever made,"
said Rabbit.
"Aren't you glad I showed you
how to do it?"
"The eggs made it very rich,"
said Squirrel.
"And you can't taste the shell at all."

"It's perfect," said Owl.
"I set the oven just right."

"Thank you all for your help,"
said Hedgehog.
"Next time I will try to do it
all by myself."

HEDGEHOG'S YELLOW CAKE

$\frac{3}{4}$ cup sugar
$\frac{1}{2}$ cup butter
3 eggs
$1\frac{1}{4}$ cups self-rising flour
1 teaspoon vanilla extract (optional)

Ask an adult to set the oven to 350°.
Then, butter a 9-inch round pan.
Mix butter and sugar together
in a bowl.
Add eggs, one by one.
If desired, add vanilla.
Mix in flour.

Put batter into pan
and bake for half an hour.

Eat warm with a glass of milk.

Raised in a family of ten, Maryann Macdonald has spent most of her life with children. She graduated from the University of Michigan and has worked as a waitress, a truck driver, and a welfare worker. She has written several picture books and has recently published her first middle-grade novel, *Fatso Jean, the Ice Cream Queen.* Mrs. Macdonald lives in London, England, with her husband and two daughters.

Born in Greenfield, Massachusetts, Lynn Munsinger graduated from Tufts University and the Rhode Island School of Design. She has illustrated numerous books for children, including most recently *Ho For a Hat* and *One Hungry Monster,* as well as the much loved Hugh Pine books. Ms. Munsinger and her husband live in Winchester, Massachusetts, with their two dogs. When she's not working, she likes to read, ski, and travel.